STECK-VAUGHN
PAIR-IT BOOKS

The Early Bird's Alarm Clock

Written by Claire Daniel
Illustrated by Eric Berendt

STECK-VAUGHN
ELEMENTARY · SECONDARY · ADULT · LIBRARY

A Harcourt Classroom Education Company

www.steck-vaughn.com

Marty Macaw lived in the rain forest near the monkeys.

Each morning the monkeys woke Marty up.

Marty did not mind getting up so early.

He liked eating the ripest fruit and the biggest nuts.

The other rain forest birds did not wake up so early.
So they didn't get the ripest fruit or the biggest nuts.
"Will you be our alarm clock?" they asked Marty.

Marty agreed to help the other birds.
But he forgot to tell them that he was forgetful.

The next day the monkeys woke Marty up very early.

Marty followed them and found a tree full of ripe fruit.

Marty ate and ate.

He forgot all about the other birds.

The monkeys giggled and asked, "What did you forget?"

Marty flew over the trees to wake up the other birds.
He called out as loud as he could.
"Kwah! Kwah! Kwah!"
"Time to get up!" screeched Marty.

9

It was too late.

All the ripe fruit had been eaten.

The other birds were hungry.

"I'm sorry I forgot to wake you," Marty told the birds.

"I promise I won't forget tomorrow."

The next morning the monkeys woke Marty up early.

He followed them to a nut tree and ate the biggest nuts.

The monkeys laughed because Marty forgot again.

The laughing made Marty remember the other birds.

Then Marty got a good idea.

Marty grabbed a branch and hung upside down.

The monkeys laughed louder and louder.

Their noise filled the rain forest.

Not one bird was left sleeping.

The monkeys had become the rain forest alarm clock.

After that, Marty followed the monkeys each morning.

He did tricks and made the monkeys laugh.

This made all the birds wake up bright and early.

They got to eat the ripest fruit and the biggest nuts.

None of the rain forest birds ever slept late again.